The Journal

Let the journey begin...

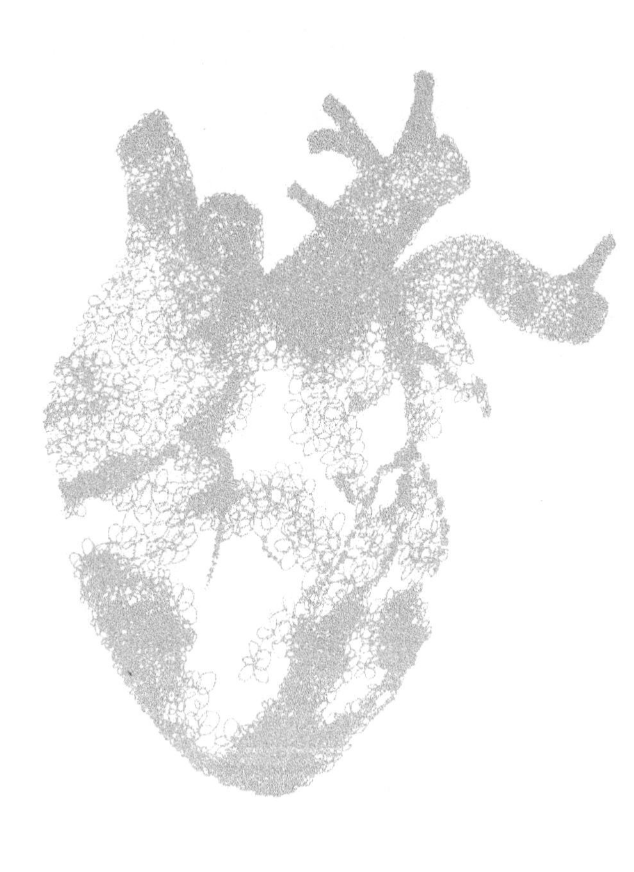

The Invitation for your heart:

Come away with Me through the sea and through the darkness,
come away with Me through the grass and gleaning pastures.
Come away with Me beyond the shadows and piercing glances,
come away with Me to the measure of all the dances.
Come away with Me to a place of no despair,
come away with Me to assert and declare.
Come away with Me beyond the shadows of all doubt
come away with Me I'll help you work it out.

Date:
What Step am I currently navigating?

"And they overcame him by the blood of the Lamb and by the word of their testimony, and they did not love their lives to the death." Revelation 12:11

"Catch us the foxes, the little foxes that spoil the vines [of love], for our vines have tender grapes."
Song of Solomon 2:15

"I WANT
YOU TO
SPEAK

"FATHER, I STEP THROUGH THE VEIL IN FAITH AND TRUST. I COVER MY LIFE UNDER THE TESTIMONY OF THE BLOOD OF JESUS."

What Step am I currently navigating?

Date:

What Step am I currently navigating?

"YOU FOLLOW ME
WHEREVER I TAKE
YOU AND YOU LIVE
LIKE YOU ARE NOT

"Enter the hidden richness and depth of your heart."

"Allow the things that give you colour, cause your eyes to sparkle, and your hair to shine to come to the surface by tilling this ground."

"I pray your potential is exposed from deep within; to fulfil your purpose, and draw the
world around you to Him!"

"EXPERIENCE
PROFOUND CHANGE,
GROWTH AND
MYSTERY, THROUGH
THE TRANSFER OF
YOUR HEART."

"No, not like this... like **this.**"

"The invitation We extended to you ten years ago can only be fulfilled
when you love Him with all your heart."

"SHH, DO NOT FEAR. YOU ARE SAFE. LOOK AGAIN. TELL ME WHAT DO YOU SEE?"

"Jesus said to him, 'You shall love the Lord your God with all your heart, with all your soul, and with all your mind.' This is the first and great commandment." *Matthew 22:37-38*

"And a second is like it: 'You shall love your neighbour as yourself.' On these two commandments hang all the Law and the Prophets." Matthew 22:39-40

"For I, the LORD love justice; I hate robbery for burnt offering; I will direct their work in truth,
and will make with them an everlasting covenant." Isaiah 61:8

"Who can understand his errors? Cleanse me from secret faults." Psalm 19:12

"Let the words of my mouth and the meditation of my heart be acceptable in Your sight, O LORD, my strength and my Redeemer." Psalm 19:14

"Come now, and let us reason together," says the LORD, "though your sins are like scarlet, they shall be as white as snow; though they are red like crimson, they shall be as wool." Isaiah 1:18

"Oh, taste and see that the LORD is good; blessed is the man who trusts in Him!" Psalm 34:8

"*Counsel is mine, and sound wisdom; I am understanding, I have strength.*" Proverbs 8:14

"Most assuredly, I say to you, unless a grain of wheat falls into the ground and dies, it remains alone; but if it dies, it produces much grain." John 12:24

"He who loves his life will lose it, and he who hates his life in this world will keep it for eternal life."
John 12:25

"If anyone serves Me, let him follow Me; and where I am, there My servant will be also.
If anyone serves Me, him My Father will honor." John 12:26

"Be sober; be vigilant, because your adversary the devil walks about like a roaring lion,
seeking whom he may devour." 1 Peter 5:8

Date:

What Step am I currently navigating?

"YOU
CAN'T
HAVE IT
BOTH
WAYS."

"This is why the evil must come out, so that We can pour in Our plans, wisdom, prudence, courage, strength, understanding, counsel, and give you success for your earthly mission."

"I AM FAITHFUL, BELOVED. YOU CAN TELL ME ANYTHING. YOU WILL NOT BE CONSUMED OR OVERLOOKED THROUGH YOUR HONESTY, RATHER YOU WILL BE LED BY ME ONTO A PATH OF REPENTANCE."

"Today your ability to build with Me will be returned. Your creative abilities will be reinstated and renewed, and your walls will begin to be repaired and restored."

"TODAY YOU
WILL BEGIN
TO KNOW YOU

"Nevertheless the solid foundation of God stands, having this seal: 'The LORD knows those who are His,' and, 'Let everyone who names the name of Christ depart from iniquity.'" 2 Timothy 2:19

"I am the One who makes you good enough, there is no other requirement. That is all.
You have nothing to add or prove My dear."

"I AM FREE!"

"I am the vine, you are the branches. He who abides in Me, and I in him, bears much fruit;
for without Me you can do nothing," John 15:5

"Acknowledgement, in My view, is the most difficult part for the human heart; but the most important as the choice to repent brings that part of one's heart back into the protection of the LORD God. This is where trade cannot occur and vulnerability is never present."

"HE IS
THE GOOD
WAY. HE IS
REST, BUT
THE HEART
MUST
CHOOSE."

"All things pertain to My sacrifice; the mercy I have established forever from the shedding of My Blood... "

"JESUS, THANK YOU. THANK YOU SO MUCH FOR ALL YOU HAVE DONE FOR ME."

"Let, I pray, Your merciful kindness be for my comfort, according to Your word to your servant."
Psalm 119:76

"You prepare a table before me in the presence of my enemies; you anoint my head with oil; my cup runs over." Psalm 23:5

"NOTHING CAN
STOP US FROM
OVERFLOWING
YOUR CUP NOW."

"IT IS THE SPIRIT OF
THE LORD INSIDE OF
YOU HUNGERING TO
WORSHIP HIM."

_"See, nothing to be ashamed about – you do not love evil, you were simply unaware
of it lurking in your heart My dear."_

"You are up, Jesus is up, the Father is up, I am up… just deceived into being pulled down."

"And the LORD will make you the head and not the tail; you shall be above only, and not be beneath,
if you heed the commandments of the LORD your God, which I command you today,
and are careful to observe them." Deuteronomy 28:13

"Therefore, you shall lay up these words of mine in your heart and in your soul, and bind them as a sign on your hand, and they shall be as frontlets between your eyes." Deuteronomy 11:18

"YOUR HEART IS BECOMING THE CONTROL CENTRE FOR THE LORD. YOUR SOUL, MIND AND BODY WILL ALIGN IN SUBJECTION TO YOUR HEART AS YOU LIVE A LIFE OF HOLINESS TO HIM."

"For the LORD God is a sun and shield; the LORD will give grace and glory; no good thing will He withhold from those who walk uprightly." Psalm 84:11

"Then God said, 'Let there be light;' and there was light. And God saw the light, that it was good; and God divided the light from the darkness." Genesis 1:3-4

"Commit your way to the LORD, trust also in Him, and He shall bring it to pass." Psalm 37:5

"Therefore, whoever hears these sayings of Mine, and does them, I will liken him to a wise man who built his house on the rock: and the rain descended, the floods came, and the winds blew and beat on that house; and it did not fall, for it was founded on the rock." Matthew 7:24-25

"HE IS THE
FOUNDATION."

"You know all of this, the promise, the outcome? Do you believe it, trust it to be true?"

"I agree you have come so far, but now the endurance given only by Me, the Spirit,
will keep you moving forward."

"Renouncing and repenting ravishes His heart because this shows you trust Him and believe
that He will do all He has promised you!"

"Your lips are like a strand of scarlet, and your mouth is lovely. Your temples behind your veil are like a piece of pomegranate." Song of Solomon 4:3

"It's all about the heart, isn't it? My heart is worth so much to Him, to You, to Father God, because that's where His Kingdom is built. It's built in me, in people, His temple."

"DO YOU HAVE
SOMETHING
FOR ME?"

"*Listening and learning under His judicial system gives you the authority and protection you were created to function with. The building of His Kingdom within you is accelerating; it is alive and strong.*"

"THE PHYSICAL BODY
RESPONDS WITH REST WHEN
THE KINGDOM GROWS WITHIN
THE HUMAN HEART AS IT
IS BROUGHT BACK INTO ITS
CREATIVE STATE. THE HEART
REMEMBERS WHO MADE IT, THE
HEART REMEMBERS WHERE IT
IS FROM; AND AS THE KINGDOM
EXPANDS WITHIN IT, THE EYES
OF THE HEART INSTRUCT THE
BODY TO ENTER KINGDOM
REST. IT IS FINALLY RELEASED
TO GIVE THE ORDER AND HAS
THE AUTHORITY TO INSTRUCT
THE SOUL, MIND, AND BODY TO
FUNCTION AS IT WAS CREATED
TO FUNCTION."

"But those who wait upon the LORD shall renew their strength; they shall mount up with wings like eagles, they shall run and not be weary, they shall walk and not faint." Isaiah 40:31

"You have removed yourself from areas of toil and exchanged them for the ability to soar like an eagle through trusting and enjoying His Justice."

"*Looking unto Jesus, the author and finisher of our faith, who for the joy that was set before Him endured the cross, despising the shame, and has sat down at the right hand of the throne of God.*" Hebrews 12:2

"HOLY SPIRIT, BE MY GUIDE, EXPOSE THIS AND BRING IT TO THE LIGHT. IT'S TIME I WAS HONEST WITH MYSELF AND WITH YOU, WITH ALL OF YOU."

"Will You hold my hand, Holy Spirit?"

"Do you see? They are gone. Finish what you started Beloved. Do not be afraid."

"For God so loved the world that He gave His only begotten Son, that whoever believes in Him should not perish but have everlasting life." John 3:16

"You have some questions?"

"But let him ask in faith, with no doubting, for he who doubts is like a wave of the sea driven and tossed by the wind. For let not that man suppose that he will receive anything form the Lord; he is a double-minded man, unstable in all his ways." James 1:6-8

"This journey of acceleration brings you into a place of trust, a beautiful and honourable trust.
A trust where you are not afraid to be who We created you to be. A trust where you are
no longer afraid to exist and live with Us in the land of the living."

"Behold, I send the Promise of My Father upon you; but tarry in the city of Jerusalem until you are endued with power from on high." Luke 24:49

"I AM THE
PROMISED ONE"

"Then you shall call, and the LORD will answer; you shall cry, and He will say, 'Here I am.' If you take away the yoke from your midst, the pointing of the finger, and speaking wickedness." Isaiah 58:9

"PEACE IS ONLY
AVAILABLE IN HIM
AND NOWHERE ELSE
WHEN IT SEEKS

"I want to fulfil my scroll, I want my inheritance upon the earth, I want Him to have His full reward from my life upon the earth. Everything He paid for with His Blood, His sweat, His tears. I want Jesus to have it all."

"Remember, this is a process of acceleration, like an intensive. I know it seems hard at this time, but you will reap the rewards. We promise."

"YOU WERE MADE FOR SO MUCH MORE THAN THIS. THE DESIRE TO SERVE THE LORD AND EXPAND HIS KINGDOM ON THE EARTH MAY ONLY BE DONE THROUGH A HEART THAT DOES NOT DESPISE HIS WORD. HONESTY AND TRANSPARENCY WITH US IS THE ONLY WAY TO RECEIVE THE FULL BENEFITS OF MERCY, GRACE AND FORGIVENESS. HE IS FAITHFUL TO FORGIVE WHEN YOU BRING THIS PART IN SUBJECTION TO HIS TRUTH."

"And when He has come, He will convict the world of sin, and of righteousness, and of judgement."
John 16:8

"I will give her justice for the pain of what is done today. I have paid in full for her justice."

"MY JUSTICE IS
FOR ALL WHO
ACKNOWLEDGE THEIR
SIN. MY JUSTICE
CAME TO GIVE LIFE,
NOT TO DESTROY IT.
I HAVE PAID FOR YOU
TO HAVE MY JUSTICE
IN THIS PIECE OF
YOUR HEART. I HAVE
JUSTICE FOR YOU."

"It is assigned to you and you alone."

"The thief does not come except to steal, and to kill, and to destroy. I have come that they may have life, and that they may have it more abundantly." John 10:10

"However, NOW, your purse is filled with the currency of His Kingdom. NOW you engage in abundance; the abundant life the Blood purchased for you."

"For we do not wrestle against flesh and blood, but against principalities, against powers,
against the rulers of the darkness of this age, against spiritual hosts of wickedness in the heavenly places."
Ephesians 6:12

"YOU ARE LORD OF ALL... LORD OF EVERY LIVING THING; EVERY BREATH, EVERY TIME, EVERY SEASON AND EVERY EVENT."

"*My arm is not too short to save, nor My ear too far to hear.*"

"Now, as you approach your mountain, your position of rulership upon the earth,
all things are there for the taking. The obstacles are diminishing."

"Let us draw near with a true heart in full assurance of faith, having our hearts sprinkled from an evil conscience and our bodies washed with pure water." Hebrews 10:22

"Therefore know that the Lord your God, He is God, the faithful God who keeps covenant and mercy for a thousand generations with those who love Him and keep His commandments." Deuteronomy 7:9

"You've had the ability to create since you were created."

"WE MADE YOU LIKE US.
TO BUILD AND TEAR DOWN.
SO FOR YOU, ANYTHING IS
POSSIBLE. YOUR LIFE UPON
THE EARTH DEPENDS ONLY
UPON WHO YOU CHOOSE TO
BUILD WITH AND WHO YOU
CHOOSE TO ALIGN WITH."

"The Kingdom of God within you gives your armour its light, its power.
Only you determine its effectiveness."

Date:

"You are free to live a life for Me, and fulfil your scroll, without any fear of harm from the enemy."

"You will be required to bring every part of your heart that is hovered over by Me,
to Us for reconciliation to ensure it filled with His Justice."

"THAT IS THE LIGHT SHINING FROM YOUR HEART! REMEMBER THE MAP REFLECTS YOUR HEART POSITION."

"This area is of primary importance."

"Now, therefore,' says the LORD, 'turn to Me with all your heart, with fasting, with weeping, and with mourning.' So rend your heart, and not your garments; return to the LORD your God, for He is gracious and merciful, slow to anger, and of great kindness; and He relents from doing harm." Joel 2:12-13

"Fear not, for I am with you; be not dismayed, for I am your God. I will strengthen you, yes,
I will help you, I will uphold you with My righteous right hand." Isaiah 41:10

"THAT'S RIGHT. MAGNETS
DO NOT STICK TO
GOLD BECAUSE GOLD
IS NATURALLY NON-
MAGNETIC. GOLD ACTUALLY
REPELS A STRONG
MAGNETIC FIELD. IF A
MAGNETIC LOOKS LIKE IT
IS STICKING TO GOLD, THAT
IS BECAUSE THE GOLD IS
NOT PURE AND HARBOURS
CONTAMINATES. THESE
CONTAMINATES ARE THE
MAGNETIC ELEMENTS
CONNECTED TO THE FORCES
OUTSIDE THE EARTH;
THE PRINCIPALITIES AND
POWERS!"

"I am the wise reprover, I am the gold, sent by the LORD who leads people to obtain a heart of gold; a heart filled with His Justice, His Kingdom. I have in Me the seven Spirits of God that facilitate this to take place."

"Like an earring of gold and an ornament of fine gold is a wise rebuker to an obedient ear."
Proverbs 25:12

"HE IS READY AND
WILLING TO HELP
YOU FULFIL EVERY
WORD HE HAS
SPOKEN."

"For of Him and through Him and to Him are all things, to whom be the glory forever. Amen."
Romans 11:36

"He who dwells in the secret place of the Most High shall abide under the shadow of the Almighty. I will say of the LORD, 'He is my refuge and my fortress; my God, in Him I will trust.'" Psalm 91:1-2

"There is an opposition that would prefer you not to take this gate. Focus on Me is key."

*"Do you think you can trust me to keep your feet secure?
Then you can delight in what I placed in your heart?"*

"In the beginning was the Word, and the Word was with God, and the Word was God. He was in the beginning with God. All things were made through Him, and without Him nothing was made that was made." John 1:1-3

"In Him was life, and the life was the light of men. And the light shines in the darkness, and the darkness did not comprehend it." John 1:4-5

"I SEE HIM DISCUSSING WITH ME MY MISSION UPON THE EARTH. WE ARE REASONING TOGETHER AT THE TOP OF MY MOUNTAIN."

"This is His plan and has been from the very beginning; that His children rule and reign on the mountains He has assigned to them."

"But Simon Peter answered Him, 'Lord, to whom shall we go? You have the words of eternal life. Also we have come to believe and know that You are the Christ, the Son of the living God.'" John 6:68-69

"YOUR HEART HAS
WON THIS BATTLE
OF LOVE WITH HIS
JUSTICE AND IT
KNOWS IT"

"So now this will be how you function; according to the original design of your heart.
Your heart will transfer the Kingdom through your soul, your mind and then your body."

"*And God will wipe away every tear from their eyes; there shall be no more death, nor sorrow, nor crying. There shall be no more pain, for the former things have passed away.*" *Revelation 21:4*

"Then He who sat on the throne said, 'Behold, I make all things new.' And He said to me, 'write, for these words are true and faithful.'" Revelation 21:5

"Of the increase of His government and peace there will be no end, upon the throne of David and over His kingdom, to order it and establish it with judgement and justice from that time forward, even forever. The zeal of the LORD of hosts will perform this." Isaiah 9:7

"Then God blessed them, and God said to them, "Be fruitful and multiply, fill the earth and subdue it... "
Genesis 1:28a

www.ingramcontent.com/pod-product-compliance
Lightning Source LLC
Chambersburg PA
CBHW040537170726
48295CB00012B/500